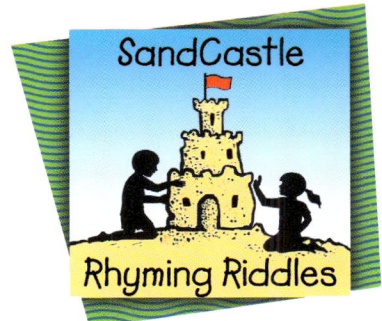

Ape Cape

Pam Scheunemann

Consulting Editor Monica Marx, M.A./Reading Specialist

Published by SandCastle™, an imprint of ABDO Publishing Company, 4940 Viking Drive, Edina, Minnesota 55435.

Copyright © 2004 by Abdo Consulting Group, Inc. International copyrights reserved in all countries. No part of this book may be reproduced in any form without written permission from the publisher. SandCastle™ is a trademark and logo of ABDO Publishing Company.

Printed in the United States.

Credits
Edited by: Pam Price
Curriculum Coordinator: Nancy Tuminelly
Cover and Interior Design and Production: Mighty Media
Photo Credits: Brand X Pictures, Comstock, Corbis Images, Hemera, PhotoDisc

Library of Congress Cataloging-in-Publication Data

Scheunemann, Pam, 1955-
    Ape cape / Pam Scheunemann.
       p. cm. -- (Rhyming riddles)
    Includes index.
    Summary: Illustrations and easy-to-read text present riddles with two-word, rhyming answers.
    ISBN 1-59197-457-7
    1. Riddles, Juvenile. [1. Riddles. 2. Jokes. 3. Reading.] I. Title.

PN6371.5.S344 2003
818'.602--dc21

2003048004

SandCastle™ books are created by a professional team of educators, reading specialists, and content developers around five essential components that include phonemic awareness, phonics, vocabulary, text comprehension, and fluency. All books are written, reviewed, and leveled for guided reading, early intervention reading, and Accelerated Reader® programs and designed for use in shared, guided, and independent reading and writing activities to support a balanced approach to literacy instruction.

Let Us Know

After reading the book, SandCastle would like you to tell us your stories about reading. What is your favorite page? Was there something hard that you needed help with? Share the ups and downs of learning to read. We want to hear from you! To get posted on the ABDO Publishing Company Web site, send us e-mail at:

sandcastle@abdopub.com

SandCastle Level: Beginning

Hink pinks

are words that rhyme and each have one syllable.

Each riddle in this book has an answer that is a hink pink.

The answers are on page 22

What do you call a coat for a chimp?

See answer on page 22

What do you call a seat for a bunny?

What do you call a cheap present?

What do you call your dog after a bath?

See answer on page 22

What do you call a tub full of numbers?

What do you call a storage space for a tiny person?

15

What is another name for a metal trash can?

What do you call lemonade that is not yellow?

What do you call an angry father?

See answer on page 22

21

The Answers

Page 4
ape cape

Page 6
hare chair

Page 8
thrift gift

Page 10
wet pet

Page 12
math bath

Page 14
elf shelf

Page 16
tin bin

Page 18
pink drink

Page 20
mad dad

Glossary

bin — a container, usually covered, for storage

chimp — short for chimpanzee

elf — a small, often mischievous creature considered to have magical powers

shelf — a thin flat piece of wood or metal attached to a wall or cupboard for storage

thrift — wise management of money

About SandCastle™

A professional team of educators, reading specialists, and content developers created the SandCastle™ series to support young readers as they develop reading skills and strategies and increase their general knowledge. The SandCastle™ series has four levels that correspond to early literacy development in young children. The levels are provided to help teachers and parents select the appropriate books for young readers.

Emerging Readers
(no flags)

Beginning Readers
(1 flag)

Transitional Readers
(2 flags)

Fluent Readers
(3 flags)

These levels are meant only as a guide. All levels are subject to change.

To see a complete list of SandCastle™ books and other nonfiction titles from ABDO Publishing Company, visit **www.abdopub.com** or contact us at:

4940 Viking Drive, Edina, Minnesota 55435 • 1-800-800-1312 • fax: 1-952-831-1632